D0089302

# WELCOME TO
# PASSPORT TO READING

### A beginning reader's ticket to a brand-new world!

Every book in this program is designed to build read-along and read-alone skills, level by level, through engaging and enriching stories. As the reader turns each page, he or she will become more confident with new vocabulary, sight words, and comprehension.

These PASSPORT TO READING levels will help you choose the perfect book for every reader.

**READING TOGETHER**
Read short words in simple sentence structures together to begin a reader's journey.

**READING OUT LOUD**
Encourage developing readers to sound out words in more complex stories with simple vocabulary.

**READING INDEPENDENTLY**
Newly independent readers gain confidence reading more complex sentences with higher word counts.

**READY TO READ MORE**
Readers prepare for chapter books with fewer illustrations and longer paragraphs.

This book features sight words from the educator-supported Dolch Sight Words List. This encourages the reader to recognize commonly used vocabulary words, increasing reading speed and fluency.

For more information, please visit passporttoreadingbooks.com.

*Enjoy the journey!*

CALGARY PUBLIC LIBRARY

MAR     2019

HASBRO and its logo, TRANSFORMERS and all related characters are trademarks of Hasbro and are used with permission. © 2018 Hasbro. All Rights Reserved. © 2018 Paramount Pictures Corporation. All Rights Reserved. Trademarks, design patents and copyrights are used with the approval of the owner, Volkswagen AG.

Illustrations by Guido Guidi and Hasbro.

Cover design by Elaine Lopez-Levine. Cover illustation by Guido Guidi.

Hachette Book Group supports the right to free expression and the value of copyright. The purpose of copyright is to encourage writers and artists to produce the creative works that enrich our culture

The scanning, uploading, and distribution of this book without permission is a theft of the author's intellectual property. If you would like permission to use material from the book (other than for review purposes), please contact permissions@hbgusa.com. Thank you for your support of the author's rights.

Little, Brown and Company
Hachette Book Group
1290 Avenue of the Americas, New York, NY 10104
Visit us at LBYR.com

First Edition: November 2018

Little, Brown and Company is a division of Hachette Book Group, Inc.
The Little, Brown name and logo are trademarks of Hachette Book Group, Inc.

The publisher is not responsible for websites (or their content) that are not owned by the publisher.

ISBNs: 978-0-316-41913-0 (pbk.), 978-0-316-41915-4 (ebook), 978-0-316-45045-4 (ebook), 978-0-316-45046-1 (ebook)

Printed in the United States of America

CW

10  9  8  7  6  5  4  3  2

Passport to Reading titles are leveled by independent reviewers applying the standards developed by Irene Fountas and Gay Su Pinnell in *Matching Books to Readers: Using Leveled Books in Guided Reading*, Heinemann, 1999.

# TRANSFORMERS
# BUMBLEBEE

## A New Car for Charlie

Adapted by Trey King

Illustrations by Guido Guidi and Hasbro

Directed by Travis Knight

Produced by Don Murphy & Tom DeSanto,
Lorenzo di Bonaventura and Michael Bay

Ⓛ Ⓑ
**LITTLE, BROWN AND COMPANY**
New York   Boston

Attention, TRANSFORMERS fans!
Look for these words while you read
this book. Can you spot them all?

running

karate

radio

distract

Bumblebee is trying to escape
from people who think all
robots are bad!
He is very brave.

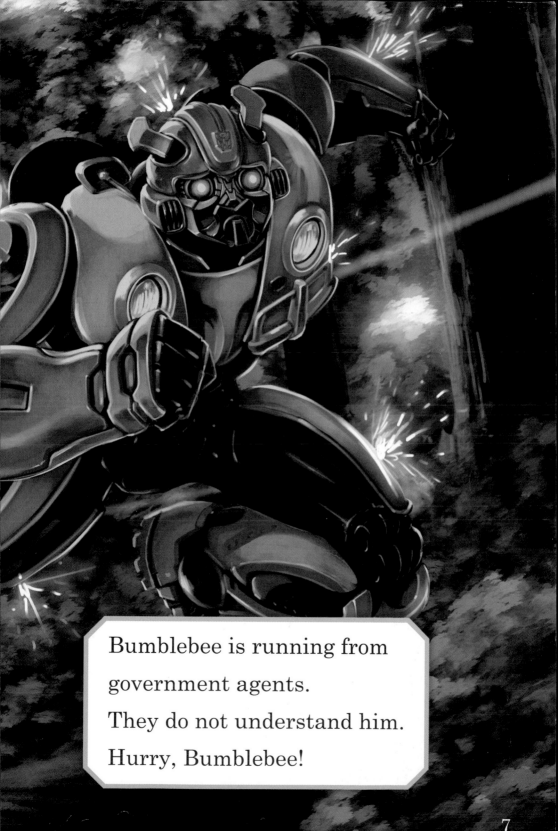

Bumblebee is running from government agents.

They do not understand him.

Hurry, Bumblebee!

Bumblebee gets out of the forest.
He runs into a Decepticon,
who also wants to capture him!
He has to fight!

Bumblebee is losing energy.
He turns into a car before
going into hiding.

Charlie Watson lives in California.
She lives with her mom,
her stepdad, her brother,
Otis, and their pet dog.

Tomorrow is Charlie's birthday.
She just wants money so she
can buy parts for her car.
Her mom says no.

Charlie goes to work.
But first she has to drop
off Otis at karate class.

It would be much easier if she had a car.
Since her parents will not give her one,
Charlie has to work for money.

Charlie serves fast food.

She does not like her job.

Charlie spills food on the
cool kid from school.
She gets upset and runs off.

After a horrible day,

Charlie goes to the junkyard.

Today, she finds something new.

It is an old car that might still work.

Charlie decides to take it home.
She makes a deal with the
owner of the junkyard:
If she can drive the car home,
she can keep it.

The car is in pretty bad shape.

It is dirty and beat-up.

Charlie cleans it.

She is great at fixing cars!

The car is clean now, but still broken.
A part falls off, but it looks like an arm.
Charlie thinks this is pretty weird
and tries to fix it.

The car changes into a robot!
The Autobot stands tall over Charlie.
She is about to yell when Bumblebee
stumbles backward.
Bumblebee is more scared of
Charlie than Charlie is of Bumblebee!

Charlie will not hurt Bumblebee. Instead, she wants to help him. She even helps fix some of his broken parts and pieces, and gives him a brand-new radio.

Charlie has earned Bumblebee's trust.
Before long, they are friends.
Bumblebee likes the same stuff Charlie
likes, including dancing, games, and TV.

Uh-oh!

Charlie's neighbor Memo
discovers Bumblebee, too!

Luckily, he reads a lot of comic books.

He thinks robots are super cool!

The three become fast friends.
But they cannot let anyone
else find out about Bumblebee!
Not even Charlie's mom can know.

One day, Bumblebee and
Charlie go to the beach.
Oh no!
Kids are playing at the beach!
They almost see Bumblebee
in his robot form.
Charlie and Memo have to
distract them.

Meanwhile, two meteors crash
to Earth.

But they are not really meteors. . . .

They are the Decepticon Rangers
known as Shatter and Dropkick.
They are looking for Bumblebee.

Being found would be very
dangerous for Bumblebee.
But he is having a hard time
staying hidden and makes
a huge mess in Charlie's house!

Dropkick and Shatter are
coming to find Bumblebee.
But he is not alone.
With Charlie by his side,
Bumblebee can face anything.